Peirene

ALOIS HOTSCHNIG

*TRANSLATED FROM THE AUSTRIAN
GERMAN BY TESS LEWIS*

Die Kinder beruhigte das nicht

AUTHOR

Alois Hotschnig, born in 1959, is one of Austria's most critically acclaimed authors, eliciting comparison with Franz Kafka and Thomas Bernhard. He has written novels, short stories and plays. His books have won major Austrian and international honours, such as the Italo-Svevo award and the Erich-Fried prize. *Maybe This Time* was first published in German in 2006.

TRANSLATOR

Tess Lewis has been translating from German and French for two decades. For her translations of Peter Handke, Alois Hotschnig, Pascale Bruckner and Philippe Sollers she has been awarded PEN Translation Fund grants and an NEA Translation Fellowship.

MEIKE ZIERVOGEL
PEIRENE PRESS

I love Kafka and here
we have a Kafkaesque
sense of alienation
– not to mention
narrative experiments
galore! Outwardly
normal events slip into
drama before they
tip into horror. These
oblique tales exert a
fascinating hold
over the reader.

First published in Great Britain in 2011 by
Peirene Press Ltd
17 Cheverton Road
London N19 3BB
www.peirenepress.com

First published under the original German title
DIE KINDER BERUHIGTE DAS NICHT
by Kiepenheuer & Witsch, 2006
Copyright © 2006 by Alois Hotschnig

This translation © Tess Lewis, 2011

This translation was made possible in part by a contribution from the
Translation Fund of the PEN American Center

This publication is supported by the National Endowment for the Arts

ART WORKS.
arts.gov

Alois Hotschnig asserts his moral right to be identified as the author of this
work in accordance with the Copyright, Designs and Patents Act 1988

ISBN 978-0-9562840-5-1

Designed by Sacha Davison Lunt
Typeset by Tetragon
Photographic image: Gaetan Charbonneau / Workbook Stock / Getty Images
Printed and bound by T J International, Padstow, Cornwall

Peirene

ALOIS HOTSCHNIG

TRANSLATED FROM THE AUSTRIAN
GERMAN BY TESS LEWIS

Maybe
This
Time

Contents

The Same Silence,
the Same Noise

Whenever I left the house, they lay on their jetty and when I came back, hours later, they were still lying there. In the sun, in the shade, in the wind and rain. Day in, day out, every day. There were two gardens of empty, rundown houses with a few trees and hedges between us. Reeds and driftwood were washed up along the shores. Their jetty was no different from the others. A fence of wooden planks protected them from the wind and their neighbours' eyes. A pot of lobelias sat on a shelf attached to the planks. Behind it, a plastic palm tree waved above the water. This tree belonged to the little girl one jetty over. The girl couldn't get enough of climbing up and jumping into the water, going under and resurfacing, screaming and going wild with excitement.

My neighbours seemed as indifferent to the child's game as they were to all their surroundings. Nor did anyone appear to take any interest in them. No one ever paid them any attention.

They lay so peacefully on their deckchairs and for a time I assumed they must be happy. But after a while I began to wonder if they enjoyed their sedentary lives. And with each passing day I found it harder to bear the sight of their dogged indolence.

Through my binoculars, I saw that they were younger than I had reckoned from a distance. Now they appeared not exactly young, but prematurely aged, perhaps. I wondered why these people appeared so familiar. And I wondered why I wanted to approach them, even though I never did.

Their idleness disturbed me. But they seemed content. It was as if, having found each other, they had accepted the way things were. Evidently they had already said all there was to say to each other. They never spoke, unless it was through the signs and symbols they traced in the air with their hands. Not once, however, did the woman ever glance towards where the man pointed.

They lay next to each other on their deckchairs, arms by their sides, legs bent or straight. For hours they didn't move, not even to wave away the mosquitoes or scratch themselves. Every day, every night, always the same. Their stillness made me feel uneasy, and my unease grew until it festered into an affliction I could no longer bear. At first, I had thought them part of the idyll I had come here to find, but now their constant presence irritated me. When I realized how easily one could see into my house from their jetty, I felt annoyed, caught out, exposed. Under surveillance, even. Yet I was the one who never let them out of my sight. Whenever I left the house, I looked over towards them, and if ever they weren't there when I came back, I couldn't relax until they returned. I now thought of them more frequently and more intensely than was good for me, and I began to feel that *I* was intruding on *their* territory. They made this clear to me. Or this, at least, is what I believed I could read in the man's expression whenever we caught each other's eye.

In the morning when I sat down to breakfast on my verandah, he was already staring at me. Throughout the day, not one of my movements escaped his notice. *Not once*, however, did he feel obliged to offer the slightest acknowledgement. His behaviour exhausted me, but it also impressed me. I even welcomed it, since I wasn't seeking contact either. Yet, because his eyes continually scrutinized me, I was always just on the point of greeting him. But then again I was never quite sure if he was actually looking at me or simply staring into space and so I stopped myself each time. As the newcomer, I didn't want to start off on the wrong foot with my neighbours. For a while I tried hard, no doubt too hard, to get their attention. But they gave no response. Initially I put this down to possible visual impairment, until one day I saw them waving back at someone in a boat out in the middle of the lake. Their failure to greet me was clearly deliberate. Still, I wouldn't have wanted it any other way. After all I had chosen this area and this house for peace and quiet and solitude. I had found all of this here and it did me good. But it was awful too because I wasn't used to it. And these people ended up tormenting me, even though they also only wanted to be left alone.

I drew closer to them because they rejected me. Rejection, after all, is still a kind of contact. To show them that I posed no threat, that I wasn't interested in meeting them, I drew my curtains whenever the man glanced towards my house. I even closed the shutters if I thought they might be watching me from their jetty. And yet, all the while, I knew that what I took for intrusiveness was really pure indifference. This was their way of showing me that for them I didn't exist and that, in truth, *I* was the interfering one, if there was, in fact, any interference to speak of.

This indifference was fine with me. But then again it wasn't, because I didn't understand what I could have done to deserve such a slight. When one day a storm battered our shoreline and the two of them remained motionless in their deckchairs, without even responding to my offer of help, I finally realized that becoming good neighbours was out of the question.

Not even a downpour could drag these two from their routine, which they pursued with determination as if they were fulfilling a duty.

Sometimes the man bolted out of his chair, startled, and hurried down the steps that led into the water amongst the reeds. He leant with both arms on the railing, bracing himself against some unknown danger. He stopped dead and stood there for hours on end. Once in a while, something moved in the reeds, circling and creating a whirlpool in the water. Then, suddenly and unexpectedly, he turned and headed back to his chair, where he made himself comfortable and lay still until night fell.

Behind the couple, the plastic palm swayed in the wind and the girl, laughing and screaming, jumped into the water again and again. I watched her and indulged in a secret protest against my neighbours' lethargy.

The sun rose and set. Nothing changed, only my agitation grew. I decided to observe them even more closely to calm my unease, as if I no longer had a life of my own but lived only through them. At night, every now and then, there was a sound of crying, like the whimpering of a child. It was carried by the wind from the direction of their house, then faded away, only to be heard again when I had stopped thinking about it. The sound was soft and unobtrusive, but loud enough to interrupt any conversation I might be having with a guest, who, from that moment, would listen intently for that strange noise.

I didn't want to talk about it and I couldn't explain it, so I would leave the room under some pretext or other every time the sound started. Either that or I would noisily rearrange the glasses to cover this whimpering.

Every once in a while, my neighbours also had a visitor. A young man lay with them on the jetty. There was a hustle and bustle the night before as they set up a third deckchair. Then the man swept the jetty with a broom while the woman settled herself and lay still just as she always did. The man spent hours scything the reeds that had grown up between the boards. After that, he stepped down into the water and swept the bed below the surface, then climbed back out and disappeared. After a time he returned with a rake and went into the water again and gently raked the reeds, carefully rearranging anything the wind might have tangled.

Raking the reeds seemed to calm him. When the young man lay with the couple on the jetty the next morning, he was placed between them. The young man lay on his back while they lay facing him, until they turned away. Not a single word more than usual was spoken. There was only the creaking of the chairs, nothing else until evening. Then the young man left.

The more absorbed I became with my neighbours and the more my life merged into theirs, the fewer visitors *I* had. If one of my friends asked about them, I found it hard to remain calm and respond appropriately. I was too preoccupied with them and afraid to expose them to the curiosity of others.

I distanced myself from the few friends who hadn't already given up on me. I never went out any more. If a friend's visit couldn't be avoided, it was agony for me not to talk about my neighbours and follow a different conversation.

I began inventing stories about them to make their idleness more bearable, personal histories that might explain what had brought them to their current state, lying there before me on that jetty. The stories became more inventive as my own life grew increasingly monotonous. Eventually I had to admit that for a long time I had been lying there with them on the jetty, and that my pretended busyness and feigned familiarity with these people was simply an attempt to escape my own life.

My attitude clearly had to change. But I didn't know how to get away from these two. I simply didn't exist for them, and that is how they hooked me. They refused contact, yet they willingly exposed themselves to me. I had caught the scent of their lives, which obviously had reached some sort of premature end. I had fed on them, devoured them, and now I wanted more. I couldn't resist absorbing their most fleeting emotions as my own, and so I carried them inside me and I lived out their disquiet, which was also my disquiet.

I protected myself by writing everything down, by recording whatever I observed, when they went into the water and when they left the jetty. I noted it all down. Finally I began taking pictures of them. Now I could look at them at night too. This way they were always available to me.

I spent most of the time on my jetty and in my boat and in the rooms inside my house which gave a clear view of them. The reports on their daily routine complemented my own. They lay on their deckchairs, I paced back and forth at home watching them. The more I learned about them, the less I was able to tear myself away.

Ashamed at first, I only photographed them furtively from inside my house. I didn't want them to see what I was doing. Then I swam along the shore, each time venturing a little closer. They didn't seem to mind, although it was impossible that they didn't notice me. But they let it happen. They pretended they simply didn't see me, even when I rowed past and took pictures of them from my boat.

Before dawn, the man brought out the pot of lobelias and set it on the shelf. He plucked the wilted leaves and flowers and scattered them expansively over the lake. Then he brought out the deckchairs and placed them in their proper positions, and the woman covered them with blankets so that the jetty became an altar. The sun rose and the woman lay down on her chair, where she would spend this day too, and the man went down the steps into the water and waded through the reeds. After a while, he took a rake into the water and moved it back and forth over the bed of the lake as if he were ploughing a field. He raked the ground with devotion and straightened the reeds, though a single gust of wind would undo his work. When he had finished, he disappeared and returned with a child's watering can. He filled it with lake water which he sprinkled on the pot of lobelias.

Exactly what kind of ritual I was witnessing I could not tell. Yet I was there every day, despite myself, craving the sight of it.

I constantly took pictures of them. I now wanted them to acknowledge my interest. I was determined that they should see me. This, too, they tolerated, and so I couldn't escape them. My only option was to imitate them, to let them see me copying everything they did. I cleaned and scrubbed my jetty and raked the reeds and swept the mud under the water. I pulled spiders' webs off the branches of my shrubs and pruned their withered leaves. Before, I had been a night owl, but now when they appeared at the crack of dawn, I was already lying in wait.

We looked at the same view, heard the same noises. We shared a common world and were separated by it. Great crested grebes nested in the reeds, ducks landed near them and near me. In the noise of children from the nearby swimming pool, my own childhood called to me. The same silence, the same noise. So much surrounded us, the waves, the fishermen going about their business out on the lake, and the water, the shore, the reeds. Did they see all this, I wondered, and if so, what did they make of it all?

I sat on my jetty and stared over at them, only to see them staring into the reeds. They were like two beetles that had fallen on their backs, with no desire to be on their feet again. When I left my jetty after a long day, I went into the house and closed the door behind me, and closed the shutters and the curtains, and turned off the light. It was dark and I closed my eyes but I still saw them in their spot, in the sun, in the rain, in the cold and wind, as if they had become one with their deckchairs. One day, they would lie on those chairs forever. As I lay in my bed, I thought about them lying there and, through them, about my own situation. Because no matter how obsessed I had become, I had really only stalked myself. In truth, it was myself I was now looking at, and I realized that if I kept watching them, *that* is what I would become.

Now I often dreamed of swimming out into the lake and letting myself drift away, anywhere the water would take me. I would lie amidst the driftwood, between the stones and the willows, buoyed by the waves. The water would be cold but

I wouldn't feel it, nor would I feel the stones that chafed my body and rubbed it raw. I would have no sense of anything, no sound, just the wind in the willow branches and the stillness. I would drift on the water without moving, another piece of wood among many, a log like any other, worn smooth by the stones, adrift on the current and at peace with what has been and what is.

I woke from the dream with a start and knew I had to do something. I remembered the house's previous tenant and how happy he had been to find a replacement and get away from the area. I looked him up. He was a friendly man who refused to say a word about my neighbours.

You don't have to stay, he said. You can always try leaving. I have a pretty good idea of how difficult that might be, though.

And so I was on my own again. I often considered moving away, but until I understood what kept me tied to the place and what I was seeing, I couldn't leave. That much, in any case, was clear. No one would help me and I knew that I had to cope with my neighbours on my own.

For months I had wanted to swim over to their jetty. I wanted to look around the place from which these people held such sway over me, to lie on their deckchairs and to see it all from their perspective for once. I decided to do it. I climbed into the water and made my way through the reeds. Dawn had not yet broken, and in the darkness I realized how badly I had misjudged the distance. I kept sinking and stepping into holes, suddenly losing my footing. I used the reeds to pull myself up again. I felt my way, like a blind man. Every few metres, I found myself reaching through slime floating on the water, which I had never noticed before. It obstructed my way and I soon noted that it grew up from the depths of the lake. I cursed myself for pursuing these people. After all, they hadn't done me the slightest harm. But I had gone too far by now to turn back. In any case, I was determined to reach their jetty and so struggled on. When the lake bed fell away or I sank into the mud, I held on to the reeds and pulled myself back up. The more I fought and grabbed and flailed about, the more entangled I became in the slimy growth like in a net that tightened around me with every step.

I was about to shout for help, to draw attention to my distress despite the embarrassment, but at that moment I stumbled on a stone. It hurt, but at least I regained my footing. I stood still, relieved to have solid ground beneath my feet again. Gradually I freed myself from the slimy strands. I placed one foot in front of the other and finally arrived at my neighbours' jetty. For a long time I stayed in the water, waiting to see if the two of them had noticed me. But everything remained quiet. I sat down on the lowest step and gazed at the mass of vegetation that had entrapped me. The waves my thrashing had set off beat against the wooden posts. I noticed a rubber duck tied to one of them with a string. The duck kept bobbing up to the surface, bumping into the post and disappearing under water again. Finally I had reached the place that had exerted such a powerful pull over me. I climbed the steps and stood on the jetty. But I no longer felt any desire to sit on either of the chairs and I made my way home through the gardens.

I had had enough of it all now, and for a long time I was cured of the craving to creep under my neighbours' skin. But at night, in dreams, I kept swimming over to them.

After one such night I went down to the jetty. The previous tenant was sitting on the steps. He seemed to have been expecting me. Or perhaps, he simply took my presence for granted. It was hard to tell. He looked over at my neighbours, as if oblivious of me. After sitting next to him for a while, I stood up and went back into the house.

From that day on, I didn't return to the jetty. It had become *his* space, and with each day it became more completely his.

He sat there in my place and I watched him from the house. I didn't take my eyes off him. I saw how he stared over at them as they stared into the water. Then I, too, looked at them. Every day, every night, always, until now.

Two Ways
of Leaving

She didn't go the usual way. She walked more calmly and slowly than she normally did on her way home from work. He followed her. She went in and out of shops. She browsed and asked the shop assistants to show her a dress. Or she took one herself from the rail, held it up in front of a mirror, and disappeared into a changing room or behind a curtain.

In a café, she smoked a cigarette, then another, and sat musing for a while, not paying any attention to the other customers. She searched in her handbag and took out a letter that she placed on the table in front of her. She glanced over it, then read it again and again from the beginning. She put it back in her bag, stood up and left the café. She strolled on from one shop window to the next, a jeweller's, then a bookshop. She entered the bookshop and left it with one more carrier bag. She paused in front of a café, then walked on. In a children's clothing shop, she fingered the fabric of a little shirt and of a jacket and trousers. She moved on, then came back, only to turn again and continue on her way.

In the market she walked past the stalls and stands, trying the fruit. She greeted others and was greeted in return, picking up one apple after another or an orange, sniffing it, and putting it back. She bought vegetables and flowers and chatted with the stall-holders.

In the neighbouring park, she sat on a bench under one of the trees and watched the chess players, the couples lying on the grass, the children feeding the ducks and the elderly people from the home nearby. She held the letter in her lap, wrote something, then crossed it out and ripped the letter up with a smile.

Ducks swam towards her, hoping to be fed, but she didn't notice them. She strolled across a footbridge, then past a row of houses on the other side of the stream. She stopped at one house with a garden. She put her bags down to catch a better view through the shrubbery.

There were children playing in the garden. She watched them for a while before ringing the bell. Then she looked at her watch and moved on quickly and with determination.

She came to a colourful area, with renovated houses, and trees and fountains surrounded by flowerbeds.

He followed her through the area to a roundabout. An enormous willow, its branches reaching down to the ground, towered at its centre.

Passing a café, she said hello to a few of the customers on the terrace and crossed the street to a shop. She stopped in front of it.

A man was closing up, pulling down a metal grille over the window. He took a coat down from a hook on the wall with a long rod and carried it into the shop. When he came back out, he spoke to her. As if realizing he had forgotten something, he disappeared into the shop again to return with a package tied with string. She accepted the package gratefully. He took it out of her hands and unwrapped it. He stepped back and proudly held a figurine out towards her, turning it this way and that. He showed it to her up close and from a distance, watching her face as he did so. As he rewrapped the figurine, she stroked his cheek, then said goodbye. A moment later she was closing the door to the next house behind her. The man watched her go, checked the grille over his shop window and finally left.

People came out of the café, and others entered or sat on the terrace. In her building, too, there was coming and going, the door opening and shutting with a sound he liked.

Under the cover of the willow he looked up at her flat. It was still too bright to expect a light to go on inside. Nor did she come to the window to look down at the square. But the front door finally opened and she emerged onto the street. She wore the dress she had held up in front of a mirror in one of the boutiques. Under her arm, she carried the figurine. She waved to someone on the terrace. She crossed the street towards him and passed him and the willow and walked down the street in the direction she had just come.

Used Goods was written on the sign over the shop door, *Gold and Silver, Bought and Sold*.

Wine glasses and vases and chandeliers filled the shop window. Tableware and cutlery. Behind them, in the shop itself, were tables and cupboards and display cabinets with glasses, goblets and mirrors. Rhinoceroses and elephants. Flower vases and crosses, a Madonna, rosaries and belts.

He scanned the names listed at the entrance to her building and pressed several buttons. The entry buzzer sounded without anyone asking his name. His hand on the railing, he climbed the stairs. On the ground floor, a dog started barking. A door opened and closed again.

The key to her flat lay in a box used for newspapers.

He had smelled fresh paint from the landing. The flat had been repainted. But the pictures on the walls, the dresser, the wardrobe and the mask above it, and the chest of drawers in the hallway with the telephone and the photographs on the wall behind it, and all the drawings, the figurines – they all seemed to be in their places.

The answering machine showed three new messages. He briefly ran his finger over the flashing light. The courtyard with its lime tree opened on to a park. The sparrows took dirt baths in the hollows they had formed. The wind swayed the swing that she had often watched from her window.

He opened the window and on the sill saw the blackbirds' nest he had found one morning under a tree and had placed on the swing for her.

Over the tops of the trees, the view extended all the way to the end of the park, to the pond, which they had often circled on their walks, and to the boat they had frequently passed but never used, saving that particular excursion for another time. Since then he had sat in the boat many times, looking over at her flat, making up for the boat trip they had never taken.

The smell of freshly baked bread drew him to the kitchen, where everything had been prepared for dinner. On the table stood two glasses and an opened bottle of wine amidst pans and plates and fruit and vegetables and meat.

On the sideboard lay the flowers from the market. He put them in a vase with water and read a note listing the day's schedule. The names and addresses were written in a hand that was not hers.

On the side of the stove, arranged in a sort of cone shape, were several of the stones they had collected on hikes along the river or brought back from trips. He had often warmed his hands with them. One after the other, he held them and thought of the places they had come from.

Photographs of children being hugged or kissed or held out to another adult were taped on the glass panes of the dresser. On the door out to the balcony, the angels painted by the previous tenant's son had been replaced with beetles. They were no doubt meant to kill the flies.

From the balcony he looked down on the street he had taken to get to work. In the distance a traffic light turned red, and he remembered how she had stood at this light and he had crossed it in the other direction so that he could turn around and watch her from a distance. The light had stayed red for a long time. She had waited, lost in thought, and he had said to himself, she's the one.

The bedroom door stood ajar. He closed it.

Footsteps approached in the corridor, stopped and withdrew again.

There was a pile of letters and some were from him and some of these were unopened. He opened them and laid them, unread, next to the others and near the pictures he had drawn of her when thinking about her or speaking with her on the phone.

There was also a box of photographs. He rummaged through them and took pictures out of the box and returned them without looking at them. Then he took them out again and examined them more closely. The photos dated from their time together, yet he didn't appear in any of them.

The phone rang. He had his hand on the receiver when the answering machine came on and he could hear the sound of hesitant breathing.

The more recent pictures were of people he didn't know. They weren't always the same people, but some reappeared frequently, showing their varying degrees of intimacy with her. Most were of celebrations – birthdays, Christmas, Easter – or were taken on holiday on different coasts, always in places that had once been theirs. They showed her leaning against a tree or with her head framed by the branches, at a concert or in an art gallery she had discovered. From the variety of places and people in the pictures, you could tell how much time had elapsed, and he noticed how much her face had changed. In many of the pictures he only recognized her after scrutinizing them carefully. But he avoided looking into her eyes. He remembered how he had once wanted to take a picture of her and how long he had waited for a moment when she didn't look tense and how difficult he had made things for himself because the child in her arms refused to wait any longer and wanted to be photographed immediately. He put the photos back in the box and looked at all the pictures up on the wall, expecting to find himself in them. But only the same faces he had just encountered in the photos from the box looked back at him from the frames.

He didn't recognize many of the places, but some of them he did associate with her – a lake, a forest clearing, a meadow – places he thought were known only to the two of them. However, there she was, reclining or standing with others in these places, laughing and serious and mischievous, alone or with someone or in a group.

He let his gaze wander, again and again, from person to person, looking for her or for the one whose eyes she sought. One picture showed the two of them in a group. They looked startled, as couples always are in such situations.

Water dripped in the bathroom. He followed the sound and sat on the side of the bath.

Drops fell from the shower head. She had taken a shower before leaving the house. He turned the tap on and off, and on again, and held his hand, and then his arm, under the stream of water. He looked at the dress she had worn to work and thought of a time they had gone to the zoo, when they had seen a lamb being born. She had drawn his attention to it, calling him by the wrong name.

It was dark now. He turned on the light and then switched it off when he realized that it could be seen from outside.

Perhaps she was out there just then, perhaps she was crossing the park or sitting in the café, looking up towards him, right now, at this moment. Perhaps she had been doing so the whole time, just as he had often done when he had arranged to meet friends at the café so that he could sit with them on the terrace. But in truth it was only to be near her or simply watch the light in her window go on or off.

He often followed her right up to her house. He watched her go through the door and disappear inside. He sat beneath the willow or in the park waiting to see if she would come to the window and pull the shades or open the window and smoke a cigarette, looking down on the square or over to the playground, the swing or the boat, wherever.

Once he actually passed the house and, by chance, looked up as she stood by her window. For a second he thought she had waved to him or made a sign. But since he couldn't be sure whether it was meant for him or not, he continued on his way without looking back.

He had been drawn to the places they had shared and had returned to them again and again. But that was years ago.

The phone rang again. An irritated man's voice on the answering machine asked how much longer she intended to keep him waiting and whether he should come up to her flat.

She didn't come and at this stage surely wouldn't. It was impossible to say what she had planned for him or why she had wanted him to see what he had seen here.

She had rung him a few days earlier. Her voice had been clear and matter-of-fact, as it always was when she was nervous. She had asked him to come at the exact time when she was out of the house.

One day he left, without planning and for no reason. She didn't ask why. She just let it happen.

The phone rang again. It stopped after the first ring. There was the smell of fresh paint and bread. In the bathroom the water was still dripping. He thought he could hear a key turning in the lock.

Then a Door Opens
and Swings Shut

The woman stopped me on my way to her neighbours. They were friends of mine who had invited
me to visit. She waved me over to her house next door
to theirs. From a distance, she had probably mistak-
en me for someone she knew. That, at least, is what
I thought. Yet, even in her living room, she looked
at me as if I were a long-overdue guest. Whenever I
took a step back, she came closer again. And even
though she seemed somewhat confused, I could sense
how keenly she watched my every movement.

A huge array of dolls sat, lay and stood on shelves
that lined the walls and jutted out into the room, as
well as in niches set at regular intervals. On the sofa
and all over the floor too, the dolls stood and lay in
a jumble, old and new, clothed and naked, but all
of them intact. Young, middle-aged and old. A few
of them seemed to take pride of place. They sat on
their own seats or in their own spaces. Set apart,
they stood out from the crowd.

My children, the woman said. Reaching for them
one after the other, she hugged them briefly, then

returned them where they belonged. They all made something of themselves, she said. Each one is successful. *Salon Annie, Salon Elly, Salon Gerda.* And they're all here with me. She sat down on the sofa and combed their hair with a clothes brush.

I stood watching her for a long time until she asked me to sit down too. Grooming her children distracted her, but every now and again she looked at me, steadily and attentively, sympathetically even, and with a level of scrutiny I hadn't experienced for ages. She couldn't really have been interested in me. After all she seemed to think I was someone she knew well, someone who was close to her, someone she was seeing again after a long absence.

The affection in her gaze was hard to bear because I had already decided to leave.

We sat facing each other silently for a while. Then she said, I'll get Karl. Isn't that why you're here?

I had no idea what she was talking about, but she obviously didn't expect an answer. She stood up and walked out of the room, leaving me alone, surrounded by all her dolls. I heard furniture being pushed aside, chests being opened, and now and again the creaking of a cupboard door or window. She left me alone for an uncomfortably long time, alone with her dolls. I considered the best way to escape without offending her unduly. After all, I was expected elsewhere.

Just then I heard her through the door. Karl would never forgive me if he missed seeing you. I don't want that responsibility, you understand. He's been waiting for you such a long time, ever since he was a child. All these years he has been asking and asking for you.

I got up and leaned against the door to hear better.

Why did you leave him, she said, he's always asking me that. *I* certainly can't explain it. He waited all this time, and now, finally, here you are. He's just getting ready for you, she said. You know, in the end he didn't believe me any more. He didn't believe in you either. Believe in you being there *for him*, I mean.

For a moment there was silence in the room and I already had my hand on the doorknob when the woman returned. She was holding a doll in her arms like a child. She came over to me and took me by the hand. She looked at me in embarrassment, but not without a certain pride. Then she led me back to the sofa, sat down and asked me to sit too. I took the chair facing the sofa. I had no idea how I would ever escape.

This is Karl, she said, and gently stroked the doll's hair. Without thinking, I brushed the hair off my forehead in a matching gesture. Look at his face, she said.

The doll had my name. And now, as the woman drew my attention to the doll's face, I noticed how much it resembled me.

He'll come back one day, I always told him, she said straightening the doll's rumpled waistcoat. He will somehow have to come to terms with you. Why you left him and why you are here now, she continued. It's a bit much for him. That's why he's not saying anything. But you'll get used to each other. It's not always easy with him because he keeps asking questions. She suddenly stopped and stared into space, staring right through me as if I were no longer there.

My name is Karl, I said, but the woman didn't answer. I didn't know how to handle the situation or how to deal with my new *friend* – a friend I was obviously starting to accept.

He's not a bad kid, she said. Peculiar, yes, but you already knew that and, let's face it, you're all he's got. And he's been waiting ever since you abandoned him. That's when he came to me. *He* can't talk to you about it, at least not yet. But things will work out now you've finally come back. And now I'll leave the two of you alone, she said, and stood up and left the room.

She had sat the doll on the sofa, right where she had been sitting. I noticed it looked exactly like me and wore the same clothes. It sat facing me on the sofa and stared me in the eye with interest. I was tempted to reach out and touch it, but at the same time I recoiled from it.

The resemblance was already striking, but it seemed to increase the more I looked.

Karl, I thought. The little fellow had my name. I looked him in the eye and at that moment remembered how, when I was a child, my mother would call me by my brother's name whenever she was upset or wanted to punish me. Over the years I had got used to it. Now that she was in a nursing home, she did it often, and it was hard to tell if this was a slip of the tongue or if she really took me for my brother.

This memory recurred as vividly as if I were experiencing it for the first time. A noise in the next room startled me, and I suddenly realized how late it was. I had completely lost track of time. I called out and knocked on the door but there was no sound of movement behind it, so I wrote a quick note promising to return, placed it on my double's lap and finally left the house.

It was too late to visit my old school friend, and in any case I no longer felt in the mood. Not after this. The woman obviously had no family and was lonely and forsaken. No matter how much she told me about her children, I didn't believe a word. That is until I crossed a few streets and passed a *Salon Annie* that I had never noticed before, and then, a few streets further on, read the name *Salon Elly* on a hairdresser's window. I was no longer so sure. In the following days and weeks I couldn't forget the old woman. I kept remembering her even in situations that had nothing to do with her. It became harder and harder for me to resist the temptation to go back and see her, as I had promised to do. I felt sorry for her and assumed that was why I couldn't stop thinking about her. But I soon realized that I also wanted something from her. After all, I had been in her house when I saw myself, through *Karl*, in a way I had never done before. And it was this encounter that drew me irresistibly to her. I thought of her at every conceivable opportunity. If I saw an old lady being helped down from a bus, I thought of her and how she could probably no longer drive anywhere alone. Or in the café, when the woman at the next table smiled at me, no doubt because she had seen me watching her. She had only just managed to catch the ring she had been toying with before it slipped out of her fingers. Embarrassed, she flashed me a smile which I returned, though I was really thinking of the old woman sitting at home surrounded by her dolls and holding Karl on her lap. I couldn't decide if Karl belonged to her or to me.

I didn't mention a word of this to my wife. I kept the encounter to myself because it was too personal to risk sharing with anyone else. At least not before I had a chance to get to the bottom of it. I contacted my school friend and apologized for not coming the other day, angling for another invitation, so that I had an excuse to walk past the woman's house again.

From the moment I arrived at my friend's, I found that he and I were as distant as we had been at school. I wondered why he had invited me in the first place. His wife tried hard to make up for his aloofness towards me, until I mentioned their neighbour. Then she, too, gave me the cold shoulder. The younger of their two daughters, who up to that point had sat close by me, every now and again casually brushing against me, moved away and refused to go to bed because she was afraid of *the mean lady*, as they referred to her. Whenever my friend and his wife got the girl to her bedroom door, she screamed and resisted with all her might. One or the other of the two girls was constantly coming into the room to be comforted by their mother, but also so they wouldn't miss a word of what we might be saying about the old woman. She stands at her window all day, watching from behind half-drawn blinds everything that goes on outside, my friend's wife explained. She can see everything from there, she said, and the children are afraid of her because she keeps luring them into her house. She frightens and upsets the children so much that you can't get a word out of them.

Today she was looking at us again, one of the girls said. She was looking in here, into my room, she said, crawling onto her mother's lap, holding onto her arm and not taking her eyes off me.

You know that's not true, her mother said. No one can see into this room, not from over there. She tried to calm the child by telling her that the woman would soon be moving away since her house was listed for sale in the newspaper. Besides, she had no one who cared for her, and desperately wanted company. That didn't reassure the children, so my friend's wife promised to speak to the woman in the next day or two.

Now I really wanted to find out what was going on. Over the next few days I went and stood in front of the woman's house several times, only to turn back each time without even entering the front garden. I always brought flowers. Then one day I was standing outside her house again and was about to give up, but this time she saw me and waved from her window on the second floor. I had trouble opening the heavy gate into the front garden and decided it must be impossible for the woman to leave the property without help.

She was waiting for me at the door. As before, she recognized me and invited me in. She took the flowers. Then, closing the door before I could enter, she was gone. I paced back and forth outside the door for a while, but this time I didn't need to knock to remind her I was there. The door opened as if by itself and the woman stood in the hallway holding towards me a vase with the flowers. She disappeared into one of the rooms, a different one from the one she had entered when I first met her. I followed her into the house. Again she left me alone with the dolls, but I didn't mind. Instead, I took the opportunity to look around and confirm that everything was as I remembered. And it was. The countless dolls, the shelves and cupboards, the niches. And the curtains everywhere, behind which other dolls were hidden. Even a few chests and cupboards I hadn't noticed the first time.

I passed by the shelves and reached into the cupboards. Time and again, on retrieving one of her *children*, I was relieved not to find any faces I recognized.

Most of the dolls were old and some had been better looked after than others. Some were shabby, others meticulously groomed. Some were dusty, others polished and freshly brushed. Evidently they had received different levels of care over a long period of time, but they all showed signs of frequent handling. I looked at a few of them more closely. *Annie* and *Elly* and *Gerda* I knew from my first visit. I picked them up, one after the other, and each time I was surprised at how attentively they looked back at me. However, a sense of unease grew within me and only subsided once I had found Karl among all the dolls. I realized that all along I had actually been searching only for him. He sat in his place on the sofa, looking as if he hadn't left it since our previous meeting. He sat there and looked at me pleasantly. I went up closer and leant over him. At the very moment our fingers touched, the woman came back into the room.

I sat down in my place, the place that had probably been kept for me from the very beginning, on *my* chair. I thought the woman was going to show me Karl again, but she held a different doll in her arms. She sat down and I knew this doll was also Karl, just a few years younger. He also looked like me, exactly like me, only as I had looked a few years earlier, and dressed just as I had dressed at that time.

The two of them sat before me, the three of them, actually, looking at me, looking into my eyes, and I saw myself in a clearing in a forest, standing behind myself and watching myself standing there. I see that I am not alone. Someone is standing opposite me. A woman, immobile. I don't know her, or rather, perhaps I do. She is standing opposite me and looking at me. She is rigid, transfixed, arms at her sides. Just as I am, I note. She is standing opposite me and sees me or doesn't see me. We stand like this for a long time without moving. Rigid, eyes fixed on each other. I see it all from behind, from my perspective, and see myself turning away, see my head turning and facing away, away from her. She is still standing and stays standing. I see the blades of grass and the tree trunks around us. I look at the ground and I sense something. I feel myself turning. And then I looked into the eyes of the old woman sitting across from me. She smiled. I felt exhausted and relieved and liberated. The woman looked into my eyes and didn't move. Eventually she raised her finger to her lips and signalled that I should remain silent. Then she got up and left the room and was gone for the rest of my visit.

I didn't know what I should do and had no explanation for what had just happened, but that it had something to do with me was clear, and that both repelled and intrigued me. I wanted to know more and so, from that time on, visited the woman frequently. Her house became our place. We sat there across from each other, and it always happened the same way. She sat across from me and I walked behind myself. The sensation was not completely new. Even as a child I had often had the feeling of following myself, of not letting this other self out of my sight. And this is what it was like now. I stood behind or followed myself, distant, impartial, devoid of emotion, and what I saw was both familiar, but then again not. I recognized it and knew that I had experienced it, but when the scene stopped, I couldn't understand what had occurred.

I saw this woman and the doll on her lap and I looked at the child I once was. I follow him. We're in a garden with a house and a path leading up to it. It's always the same. A door opens and swings shut. A hallway, a staircase, a room. Another place, there are many of them, a meadow by a forest, a clearing. A woman is standing in front of me, she takes a step towards me. I want to leave this place, but cannot stay away. As strange as these encounters were, I kept wanting to experience them, to relive them. I could hardly wait for the woman to disappear into one of the rooms and return some time later to show me what had been. Karl sat opposite me, in her lap, sometimes younger, sometimes older. It varied. His age was as unpredictable as the story she revealed to me.

I knew I wouldn't get any explanations, so I didn't ask, afraid she might stop the game. I accepted that she would only sit there in silence and show me myself. Everything I witnessed I relived once more, only this time I was safe, but not entirely. And however much I saw, I knew I could not interfere. The road, the house with the garden, the hallway and staircase, the room and the wall I always ended up facing. Repeating what was, to see it once again, again and always anew.

I knocked and she welcomed me. In time she opened the door before I'd even had a chance to knock, or simply left the door ajar. I entered and sat on my chair, and got ready. I sat alone for a long time, as if she were waiting until I had made myself at home. Then she came out of one of the rooms, greeted me and sat on the sofa, without a word, always the same. When it happened, when she showed me myself in the guise of the doll as I had been, it was I who was sitting on her lap, and she was the witness of what happened to me. She stroked my hair as I dived into the images, merged

with them and disappeared. She never stopped looking at me, and it was into her gaze that I fell and in
her eyes that I awoke hours later, hours that I could
not account for.

Karl was always there with us, watching me
while I remembered particular moments from my
past, places and situations into which I was about
to plunge, where all traces of my history had been
erased. It was there that I encountered myself, as
the child I once was, and I would see myself run,
or sit, or walk through the trees. The same images, always in the same sequence. This house
with its front garden, the room, the wall, always
the same, and always someone would be picking
me up, lifting me and lowering me again, lifting
and lowering me, weightless. There the memory
ended each time and I landed back in the present,
looking into the eyes of the woman who welcomed
me with a smile.

We sat across from each other, looking at each
other in silence, and I remembered, though af-
terwards I could no longer say what it was I had
recalled.

I knew very well what kept drawing *me* back to
this woman, for she had something to offer, something I accepted. But what *she* could possibly gain
from these meetings, I had no idea.

I became even more estranged from my wife than
before. She suspected I had become involved with
another woman, and while she was not wrong, it
was, in fact, *myself* I had become involved with, in
a manner I would never have thought possible.

I got increasingly used to the old woman's idiosyncrasies, but it was a while before I realized how fragile and vulnerable she was and that our time together was running out. There was so much I wanted to know, to experience and to see once again. When I awoke to her gaze she stood up and left. I then had the room to myself for a long time and I looked at the other dolls. I often wondered how many others might have sat here before in *my* seat. They had come to her over the years, those who had turned away from themselves, for whatever reason, she explained. They are here, she said, and what happened to them is here too. Some of them have visited me every day for years now. Every day, every night, in their dreams, in their sleep, they come to me, she said. They can stay here. Nothing will happen to them here that has not already happened to them elsewhere long ago.

One day I opened a cupboard in which she often rummaged in search of something. I opened it and found Karl looking at me out of many faces. The dolls that showed me as a child were scuffed and old. Their clothing was tattered and threadbare but meticulously folded or hung up. I even saw my first pair of shoes, which I remembered since I had been photographed in them so often. They were there, underneath the pullovers, shirts, jackets and trousers of long ago.

The woman always referred to her *children* when speaking about the dolls, but she didn't react when I asked her about her daughters. She frequently mentioned them during my early visits, and the next time I passed by one of her daughters' hair salons, I went in. In *Salon Annie* a woman welcomed me and took my coat. I had to wait so I sat in a corner, picked up a newspaper and observed the place. After a while I recognized the old woman's daughter because she looked like the doll I had seen just the day before. They were identical down to the last detail. She had the same voice as her mother, and when I stood in front of the doll the following morning, that voice still sounded in my ears.

Whether I liked it or not, I too had become one of the old woman's dolls, or perhaps I had always been one. She sat me on her lap, and I let it happen, because in exchange she gave me something I wanted and each time craved more deeply – myself. And so I sat across from her and observed how I, as her doll, sat on her lap and had my hair stroked and was petted and cuddled. As long as I was sitting across from her, I was happy, and it did me good. And as soon as I left her house, I was drawn back there. She knew it, or maybe she didn't. It was different each time. She was close to me but also distant. She gave me the space I needed and didn't coerce me, but every fibre of my being was drawn to her and to this place where something of me was hidden and could ultimately be found through her. So I tried to live up to any expectations she might have of me, and I enjoyed that. I felt an affinity with her, felt understood by her, and if not understood then at least accepted. I had surrendered myself to her and continued to abandon myself to her and to the images she showed me of myself. And so I returned to her every day, and before long it was as if I lived with her.

One day my wife confronted me, but it seemed to me that she didn't want to know the real reason why I had changed. I didn't mention the woman since I didn't want to destroy anything that wasn't already over. And when, the following day, I sat across from the woman, it seemed to me that she was smiling more contentedly than usual.

It was impossible to say what bound us together. We depended on each other without knowing why. When I was with her, we didn't leave the house. On the contrary, it was only deep within her house that we could truly be there for each other and be alone with each other. Alone, that is, apart from the local children who stalked her. They just couldn't leave her alone. Again and again, one of the boys would sneak into the garden and venture up to the window. Using his hands to shield his eyes, he would press his face to the windowpane to see inside. I see her, he would yell, she's inside, and he would shout, bang his fist on the glass and disappear, only to throw a handful of gravel at the house from a safe distance. Each time the woman acted as if she hadn't noticed anything, which was not possible. Once, when the children were behaving worse than usual, I went to the window and jerked it open. Some of the pebbles flew into the room and fell onto the floor and onto a doll I hadn't noticed before but in which I recognized the face of the boy who had thrown the gravel.

The children were afraid of the woman, and I noticed that with time they also grew afraid of me because they associated me with her. They avoided me when they saw me on the street or made a game of holding my gaze without greeting me. On my rare visits to my old school friend, his two daughters shrank from me like frightened animals. They hid behind chairs or behind their parents, who grew more reserved with each visit. Eventually I no longer dropped in to see them and changed my route when I came to visit my new friend.

Each time I left her house, a part of me remained behind, and I could feel its absence when I was not with her. I didn't know her at all, in fact. She was a stranger to me in so many ways. Nothing bound me to her other than her knowledge about me and her ability to reveal me to myself to an extent no one else ever could. I felt secure with her, but at the same time was unsettled by the fact that I had no idea what her intentions were or why she should take such an interest in me.

A blank wall. That is what I faced every time, that's how it begins. My eyes trace the expanse of the wall, from top to bottom, from bottom to top. Someone picks me up, lifts me, lowers me, lifting, lowering, always the same, sometimes near, sometimes from a distance, until this wakes me and I look into the woman's eyes as she holds Karl, raising and lowering him, pressing him to her, rubbing him against her body. She was doing to him exactly what I myself had just experienced. This irritated me, but, fearing she might no longer show me myself, I pretended not to notice anything.

From then on, the woman changed. More and more frequently, she sat across from me on the sofa, hugging Karl and caressing him. She stuck out her tongue, showed it to me briefly, then ran it over Karl's face. Then she showed me how she lifted the child and lowered him, raised him and hugged him tightly without once taking her eyes from me.

I stayed away for a while, forcing myself to keep my distance, yet I longed to go there all the more. I gave in, stopped resisting. I pretended nothing had changed, and she pretended nothing had changed, and we sat across from each other, as we had done before. She stroked Karl's head and looked me in the eye and placed the child's finger in her mouth, kissing it tenderly for a long time and sucking on it. She slavered over the little hand, and pulled it back out of her mouth where the fingers had begun to dissolve. The more often they disappeared into her mouth the smaller they got. They melted away and became stumps, before they finally vanished. She kept licking and sucking tenderly, and eventually put the entire hand into her mouth, which melted and vanished. She seemed fully aware of herself and of what was happening. She ate with relish as I sat there across from her and I watched as I disappeared into her. At the same time she slowly deteriorated right before my eyes. Soon enough she was sitting there all but motionless, surrounded by countless dolls grabbed at random, smiling to herself and running her fingers over the head and face of each doll before it disappeared inside her. Now when I visited her, she hid behind her smile and her tongue, which flicked out of her mouth towards me again and again, and was not directed at me any more, but at everyone.

Maybe This Time,
Maybe Now

Walter's not coming. That would be fine with us if only our parents didn't live in expectation of him. They constantly hope that he might just show up, that when we get together at their place again, the whole family might just be there, all of us, as if we did in fact belong together, as if we were a whole, one more time, or for the first time rather, because it hasn't happened yet, not once.

When I visit them and suggest, as I did last time, that we all go to my sister's house to celebrate her birthday, they're delighted because nothing is more important to them than their children. So we agree to surprise my sister the following day, and then visit my brother, maybe even my other brother, if there's enough time, since he lives a bit further away.

You know how much I like it when you are all together, Mother says, and tells me everything that has happened while I was gone, and we grow closer, become close even. After a while, however, she stops talking and remains quite still. Father says, Maybe it's better if you two go and I stay at home. Maybe

Walter will stop by tomorrow. And the next day we don't go to my sister's, since Mother doesn't like to leave Father by himself and she doesn't want to miss Uncle Walter, should he finally come, as she says. So they stay at home, in the house, and I stay with them. My sister comes to visit, to celebrate her birthday here, in our parents' house, not at hers as she has wanted to do for decades.

One of them always used to stay at home. For as long as I can remember, they've never left the house together, and for some time now they haven't even left separately, fearing that Walter might come and they wouldn't be there.

If we want to see them, we have to go to their house, and we do. There are plenty of occasions: Father's birthday, Mother's, their anniversary, my brother's birthday, my other brother's birthday (the one who supposedly looks just like Uncle Walter), saints' days, weddings and christenings, All Souls' Day and All Hallows' Eve, Christmas, Easter and Pentecost. Yes, there are occasions enough and we observe them. From all directions, we make our way to our parents' house.

Besides Walter, Father has another brother and a sister who come to every occasion, along with their sons and daughters, the cousins with their children, the nephews, my great-uncle, all of them. Well, not all of them, in fact, because Uncle Walter is always missing. The more he stays away, the more my parents long for him and the more stubborn their hope that this time, today, now, he could perhaps still come after all.

But Walter doesn't come, at least not while we are there. We don't make up for his absence, those of us who are present, and no matter how hard we try to distract them, to make them forget about Walter, it never works. The rest of us do count for something, but not enough compared with him, since Walter's absence makes us all invisible in our parents' eyes and in our own. Those who are missing are noticed, but only until they come through the door, join those who are waiting and disappear into the group. It's always the same game, who's there and who isn't, how many are we now, and who might then still come and who not.

The names of the others are mentioned. Yet it's only his name everybody thinks about. However, no one asks after him, on that we silently agreed a long time ago. Not a word is said about him. But eventually our parents start talking about him and then we speak of nothing but Walter.

In the house and in the garden, we sit together and wait, pretending that we aren't waiting. We look at each other and try to talk to each other, pretending that this is enough. But it isn't. And how could it be, waiting as we are for another, morning, noon, evening and into the night. Whether we don't mention his name once or whether we speak of nothing but him, we wait, at each and every family gathering and also the days and weeks in between, through the years and decades that our family has been around. And should we, just once, manage to be together without a single thought of him, a mere look from one of us is enough to bring us all back to him, and to our parents, for whom, once again, our presence is not enough.

With our constant glances at the door, never intended for the one coming through it, but searching for the one who is not to be found, we simply tell one another, but no, you're not Walter. It took me years before I could interpret these looks and understood that they had nothing to do with me, but with the one who was missing, always the one who was missing.

That's how it was, and it's no different now, and none of us could say why it was the way it was, the way it had to be, the way it is now. In this sense, we have always lived with Walter. We know him and don't know him. The youngest of us, in fact, have never laid eyes on him. And when photos from our parents' or another relative's childhood are passed around at the gatherings, there is never any trace of Walter.

We know him from hearsay and from our parents' stories and expectations and their invariably disappointed hopes, which have now become ours. Should a stranger come to the door or pass by a window, which happens often enough at our family gatherings, my nieces and nephews are taken aback and look at each other, checking to see if the stranger could be Uncle Walter, nodding inquiringly or shaking their heads. No, it's not Uncle Walter, for whatever reason. Uncle Walter looks different, Uncle Walter is taller or shorter, depending, since each of us has our own image of Walter. But in all the stories he's good-natured, well-meaning and attentive, and interested in all of us. That's what they tell us. But we don't believe it, just as when I was a child, for years I didn't believe he even existed. But there is a Walter. He has a wife called Ria. And she comes to our parents' house. And he has a son, too. A grandson, even. Why shouldn't he exist? He does. And he comes to visit. That's if what our parents tell us is true, as not a soul has ever witnessed these visits. In any case, after each so-called visit, our parents' lives are, for a time, off kilter.

He sends his best. He has a kind word for each of us. He promises to join us for the next gathering and looks forward to getting to know us, each and every one of us. That is what they say and that is what we hear. There are still a few of us who believe it, or pretend to for our parents' sake, but this is not to say that we all appear to believe it or that it could possibly happen one day, maybe this time, maybe now.

Walter hasn't come. Nor, on the other hand, have our parents ever gone to his house. He has never invited us children. From the beginning, Walter never encouraged visitors, and our parents always respected his wishes, or at least that's what they say.

For a long time, I wanted to get away from the family gatherings. Whenever I sat with the others in the kitchen or in the garden and the waves of noise rose around me, I thought of Walter and how calm and peaceful it must be where he is, and of how much I, too, needed to escape. And I was impressed by his rejection of us. When I got into the car, on the way there and on the way home, I thought of nothing but avoiding the next gathering and the one after, of never turning up again, because our parents and all the others needed to understand that I could no longer comply with their wishes. I decided to stay away, but still ended up coming to the next event.

And then I did leave and stayed away. For a while I didn't show up any more. But I soon realized I didn't have the strength to stay away for good, because I spent the whole time thinking about them and wondering whether or not Walter had ever come.

While I stayed away from the family gatherings, not one of my relatives mentioned my absence. This bothered me, as I felt that they should notice I wasn't there. I wanted them to miss me. After all, Father is old, and Mother isn't getting any younger. How many more times would I see them, I wondered. And so I forced myself to return.

My parents cling to this person, and we in turn all cling to him. Walter haunts them and they let it happen, and so do we, as if we had to pay off a debt or atone for some unspecified offence.

As a child, I often asked my mother what we had done to Uncle Walter to make him stay away, because I assumed we must be at fault. I sensed how easily I could embarrass her with this question and what power I had over her at that moment, and so I asked it when we were not alone, preferably in public.

What happened with him? I asked. Why do we do this? Why do we always wait, when he never comes?

Why should anything have happened? She replied. Nothing happened, not a thing. She disappeared for a while, then returned. Walter was always that way, she said, even as a child. Always apart from the others and on his own. Crowds are not for Walter, they make him anxious. There are too many of us for him, too many at once. It frightens him. He's afraid of us, she said, afraid of how loud we are now. It's true. She's right about that, we've always been loud. But why we should keep waiting for him when we've always been too many for him, to that she gave no answer.

In summer, weather permitting, we wait in the garden because the children's rowdiness often makes it difficult to stay indoors. So we sit in the sun or under one of the trees. Only Walter's chair sits off to the side in the shade of one of the other trees.

Walter can't bear the sun. Too much light isn't good for him, and draughts make him ill. So the windows and doors are all kept shut, since Walter mustn't become ill. In summer, we wait in the sun or in the shade, and in cold weather we wait indoors. The house is not heated. The warmth isn't good for Walter, so in winter we sit chilled in the rooms, looking at each other but with Walter on our minds. We try to get along, which we do and then don't. We leave only to return, looking at one another again, and we wait for Walter without really expecting him. We sit together and try to forget him, and whenever we succeed or simply believe we've succeeded, even for a moment, when things are quiet, peaceful and calm, Mother says into the silence: And when I think that things are so good for us, and Walter is alone somewhere, I don't think it's right.

Walter isn't alone. We know his wife and his son and his grandson, who are both named Walter, after him. He's not alone, we know, but we don't contradict Mother, since for her that doesn't count. For Mother, Walter was and is alone. Ria doesn't change anything, she says dismissively. We have each other, but Walter is always on his own, so we must think of him and take care of him. And that is no doubt precisely what Walter wanted to avoid.

When we exchange presents, there is always one for him, inconspicuous, but plainly visible for those who want to see it. After the Christmas tree is cleared away, one present remains unopened until Easter or Pentecost, or even later, when it disappears into a cupboard, only to reappear under the tree the following Christmas.

Once in a while, Father will suddenly stand up and go to the telephone in the hall, to enquire. Although everyone watches him, they all continue to speak, or scream, or be silent, as if they haven't noticed a thing. After a time, he comes back into the room and sits in his chair, clearly distracted. He gazes at those around him, but says nothing. The afternoon passes, and the evening, then he taps the table with his finger and announces, Walter's still coming. He says this as he glances around him. Who did you speak to? Who did you call? we ask.

Walter should be here by now, he replies. This from Walter's son, who had no idea where else Walter could have gone. And then the doorbell rings. Mother looks around, gets up and leaves the room, closing the door behind her, and we stay put.

Walter's wife occasionally stops by unannounced, whether out of consideration for our parents or because Walter sends her. The door opens and we see that Walter isn't with her. She has come without him. Still, one person fewer is missing, because Ria belongs with us, even if she doesn't count without Walter. So we wait with her, since she always insists that he intends to come. Walter will follow, she says then. She has come ahead of him because he was held up by someone at the last moment. We wait, and while waiting she becomes restless and worried, as do we and our parents. Something must have happened or he would be here, she says. She stays a while longer, then leaves. We stay behind, waiting for her call, for a sign. But there is none, ever, as if there really were no Walter, not for us.

But there is a Walter. And he's coming. If what our parents tell us is true. Walter's coming, they say. In a day or two, in a week, in a month. Walter will come in his own time. The door opens and he's standing here in the room.

Mother calls. Walter was here, she says. His chair is still warm. Imagine, we almost missed him! Good thing we had a feeling he'd come. Then she says, Next time, make sure to be here. I always knew, she says then. Walter is coming, he's looking forward to seeing you. Next time you'll come too. Walter's coming, he promised. Then we'll all be together. Promise me that you'll come. Walter would like to see you, she says. I promise, as do the others. We all promise, each of us. Yes, I promise, I say. I'll be there and Walter will too, for sure. And at our next visit they both tell us about Walter and how it all went.

We can't leave, we have to include him, they say, when they suspect that we might once again be trying to stop them thinking of Walter by suggesting an outing.

We don't want to tempt them away, so we listen to them and their stories. Eventually it's evening, then night, and although it's clear to the rest of us that Walter won't be coming this time either, they seem calmly confident, knowing they're home and ready in case he does come.

We're not so different, I often think. I, too, want to be available. I know that desire all too well. If someone is waiting for me, anywhere, or wants to stop in and see me, announced or unannounced, I sometimes think I consist of nothing but the desire to see that person. So I shy away from commitments, and whatever meetings I agree to, I cancel, just to be free in case anyone should decide to stop by. I make an exception for my parents, so often, in fact, that there is little time left for anyone else. Still, even on my way to their house, I worry that someone might be standing at my door and I won't be there. The last time I came, at the very moment I opened the door, it dawned on me that I had forgotten about Winkler. I hadn't seen him for years, and now I had forgotten about him. He was left standing at my door with his wife and children, and I couldn't reach him, no matter how often I tried, either then or since. In fairness, it wasn't the first time I had stood him up like that.

It happens time after time. And time after time while I am with my family at my parents' house, sitting in the garden or at the dinner table, my mind wanders to my front door where someone might perhaps be waiting. Then I look at each member of my family in turn and think how impossible it is to escape these family ties. No one has managed it except Walter, and for him there was a price which we all must pay.

And yet, at each gathering, the moment comes when it's time to leave, to let it go and admit that there is no point in waiting, at least this time, and Father sweeps his hand across the table and says nothing, but then, finally, he says, Walter probably won't make it today after all. He stands up and thanks everyone for coming and, turning to Mother, says, I'll be off to bed then. Mother follows him to the door of the room. She closes it behind him, and straightens her blouse and sits down and stays with us for a little while longer. Eventually she lowers her eyes, smiles and claps her hands cheerfully. Tomorrow I will give Walter your best, she says.

The Beginning
of Something

The stamps on the envelope were still moist. I noticed they were foreign. As I got to the window I realized that I was, in fact, in another country, somewhere unfamiliar. I didn't know where. To confirm or dispel my sense of foreboding, I went into the bathroom. A stranger's face looked at me from the mirror.

Finally awake, sweaty, but relieved to have remembered a dream after so long, I got up and found everything in order. I was drawn to the table where I had worked through the night. I looked out of the window and saw it was all as I remembered in the dream. A late afternoon in early autumn. Even the woman behind the half-open shutters in the bay window opposite, the woman who had watched me in my dream, she was still there and hadn't lost interest in me.

A dream, I thought, and sat on the bed to finish the dream, but everything stayed the same.

Sheets had been draped over everything in the room, I now noticed. The walls were bare. The room seemed to have been abandoned long before. I closed the curtains. Darkness fell.

Several doors led out of the room. Lock them, I thought.

They were locked. The keys were on the inside. I knew I had to get to the mirror. Only then would the dream stop. I felt my way to the bathroom. The mirror was still there.

I started to wash myself. My hands mechanically scrubbed my body and didn't stop. I wanted to escape from the dream. But I couldn't wash what had happened from my skin, and my hands rubbed myself raw with the scalding water. Finally, they pushed my head under water and only relented when I realized that I could not resist them. The hands reached for a towel and used it to cool the red face that looked out at me from the mirror, as if already used to the fact that I was another.

I pulled myself together, convinced the darkness was deceiving me. But my hands throbbed with pain, and with the pain they became mine once more. I tore open the curtains and examined my hands in the daylight. They were covered with blisters. I wrapped them in the towel, which was now no longer cool enough to soothe the burning. Before long I brought the towel to my face and held it against my forehead.

The arms weren't my arms. I looked down at myself and knew the mirror was after me again. It all happened more quickly this time, since I went along with it. The washing, the hands, just like before, my head held under water. But I let it happen, and, as if to reward me, the water was now cold.

The bay window opposite was wide open and the woman had gone, but I was still not alone.

I covered the mirror and burrowed into bed under the towels I had dampened to cool my skin. Like everything else in the room, I too was draped in sheets, and I tried to remember how things could have come to this.

It worked, or at least I thought it did. I remembered a story, my story, at least I thought it was. And the calmer I became by thinking about this story, the more sharply the pain returned, and I was pleased to be forced into alertness. The pain would pass, and I tried to distract myself by concentrating on this thought, which worked for a while, until I noticed that everything I remembered vanished the moment I thought of it, vanished permanently, as if it had never happened, as if I had never experienced it. As soon as I remembered something, I seemed to forget it. No matter what I thought. The last few hours. How I came here. There was an answer, which appeared like a familiar face in a crowd, but it immediately disappeared and was as strange as all the others.

The letter, I thought. What has been written can't disappear. The sealed envelope was on the table next to yesterday's notes.

I didn't recognize a thing. Among the sentence fragments that had been cut and reassembled without apparent rhyme or reason, the words *origin* and *downfall* appeared again and again. *Origin* and *downfall*, sometimes crossed out and rewritten, or one replacing the other.

There was no address on the envelope. I held it up to the light and could just make out some writing on the paper inside.

They can come, it said. *They can come and get me.*

The courtyard in front of the house was, in fact, a public square, I now realized, surrounded by iron railings, the paving stones bright and baking in the sun. Mothers sat on the benches. Their children ran from the shade under the trees out into the warm sunshine and back again. The window opened at the first touch and the cool breeze soothed my skin.

On one of the benches I noticed a girl who looked familiar. So did the dog licking her hand. I had already met them.

Who was to come and get me? To go where?

I didn't dare open the letter and decided to look only at the notes on the table, but first I made sure that the door was still locked.

They can come. They won't find me.

I picked random notes from the piles of paper, and the sentences on them seemed to be written just as randomly. They were unintelligible paragraphs in which I tried to defend or justify myself, though why it was impossible to tell, at least for the moment.

No one can escape themselves, I read, *there is no escape from one's self*, and I heard myself laugh in a voice that was not mine. I had escaped from myself long before.

These sentences were no help, yet some stuck with me. I couldn't get them out of my head. It was as if they might explain what had happened. But they didn't. *I am preparing my departure. I am leaving my name to the lies.*

Next to the bed was a sheet and I pulled it over the sentences with a movement that was not mine. I hadn't left, and the sentences couldn't be trusted. Nor could the noise that had been coming from the next room for some time now.

The door to that room was not completely shut, I now noticed, and a draught moved the door, opening and closing a gap. In that room, too, everything was draped in white.

No one knew I was there and I wanted it to stay that way, so I shut the door. The knob was pleasantly cool in my hand.

At this point I also became aware of a smell that had not caught my attention before, even though it was a strong one and permeated everything. It was the smell of the elderly, of medicine.

Into whose story had I fallen, I wondered. The story had as little to do with me as the smell. Just as I didn't fit here, so nothing here fit me, except for the notes, and I had no idea what I should do with them. I had covered them like everything else. The sentences were not to be trusted. *These are the facts*, they said, *there is evidence against me* and *who will believe me, no one*. Protestations followed reproaches, all sorts of claims that meant nothing to me, suppositions and self-incrimination, paragraphs rendered unintelligible.

Next door, the floor creaked.

Encounter

It raised its head and froze in this posture as if to threaten an enemy, then resumed its march again. Its carapace gleamed in the sun. Its pincers snapped audibly on nothing. Occasionally it would grip a stalk of sturdier grass with them and, as if searching for a better view of its surroundings, it would hoist itself up, only to let itself drop once it had reached the top of the stalk or the upper side of a leaf, and lay motionless on the ground. It would remain almost completely immobile for a while, then suddenly continue on its way with a violent start, or it would circle around the next stalk and burrow its head in the earth at the base, or it would turn and set off in the opposite direction. Again and again, it would stop dead, perhaps sensing a threat. Then it would struggle on, its body rising and falling, towards a cluster of paving stones set in the grass and leading to a gravel path. The carapace creaked as it scraped the stones, and the animal stumbled and fell onto its back. It jerked itself back onto its feet and crawled into the cooler grass, continuing its march. The struggle seemed to tire the animal since it frequently stopped to lie full length on a stone, and each time it took a bit longer to lift its soft, defenceless underbelly. In one attempt to push itself off a stone, it tumbled over the edge onto the gravel. Its limbs waved in the air. Its underbelly was noticeably lighter than the rest of its body. It rose and fell continuously, swelled and collapsed in on itself. An ant ran across it, briefly touched its face, its jaws, and disappeared under the pebbles. Then the ant returned and crawled over the creature's face and up to its eyes. The ant gnawed and tore at the eyes. It disappeared again and returned, biting deeper into the creature each time. The creature must have injured itself in the fall, because it was now dragging its left side. And yet, despite this handicap, it moved nimbly over the gravel, which was spread so sparsely in spots that patches of earth, the same colour as the creature, could be seen amongst the rocks. Whenever it reached one of these clearings, it tried to burrow into the ground, but soon gave up and hauled itself along towards the kerbstone from which it had fallen and which it intended to climb over. It did everything it could to get back to the grass, but its little legs foundered on the stone's smoothness. It laboured almost obsessively along the edge of the path until it found a gap in the kerb through which it could squeeze onto the lawn. There it lay still for a time and began to tend to itself. It ran its antennae carefully over the dam-aged limbs and brushed them across its mouth. Its mandibles moved back and forth as it crouched and stretched. With a jerk it managed to flop onto one of the stones, but landed on its back. A violent trembling shook its hind legs and spread through its whole body, then abated, growing calmer until it subsided completely. Meanwhile the shovel-like forelegs banged wildly against its head. Its mouth opened and closed ceaselessly, as if begging, and its underbelly collapsed and stayed flat. Its lustre was gone except where the ants were at work. They had come out of the grass in droves and swarmed over its body. The forelegs had stopped banging and hung motionless in the grass. Its mouth was wide open. The ants crawled in and out and made off with their booty. They nibbled and gnawed at the body and hollowed it out until it was light enough. Then they carried the husk away.

The Light
in My Room

I turned off the light and looked out towards the island. I heard someone calling, but I could not see that far in the darkness. After a while, lights flashed in the reeds, and I could finally make out the man whose voice I had been hearing for hours. From his boat, he shone a light into the reeds, where I now saw something white floating back and forth across the water. It always returned to the circle of light, like a person trying to get to shore. In fact, it was just a piece of cloth, perhaps a vest belonging to one of the children I had seen on the island that afternoon. The man kept shining his light on it, but didn't pull it out of the water.

I remembered how they rushed back from the island in their boat, and the minute they set foot on land, they disappeared into their houses without the usual hue and cry that spread through the area whenever they returned.

They made their way from a spit of land through the reeds and out to the island. It always took a while before they could be seen again in the undergrowth, since they had become so adept at disappearing into the landscape. Whether any sound from the island reached me depended on the direction of the wind.

They were a gang of children from the area, not many and not always the same ones. It was hard to say why they were so drawn to the island. They went there often, almost daily, even though access to the island was prohibited, because of the few protected species that nested there.

They took sticks and poles with them in the boat, and apples, which would end up floating, a few days later, in the water near the reeds.

They played at being hunters in the reeds. With their sticks and poles, they waded in the mud along the shore, and frightened animals shot out of their holes and escaped out over the lake. Then they rowed to the island, and, depending on the wind, either a slapping beat of oars could be heard, or silence. This silence drew me to the window more often than any of their yelling.

When they headed back or were on their way over, they made sure they were safe from prying eyes, and if they realized they were being watched, they waved cheerfully and headed off in another direction. There was no use in taking it personally, since everyone here had sneaked onto the island at one time or another.

The light was still shining in the reeds and the man poked at the water with a hook.

I drew the curtains, knowing perfectly well what there was to see. The man himself had made sure of that. I thought of him often and in dreams I climbed into his boat and he rowed me out to the island. Now he was at it again. A vest floating in the water, a piece of cloth that had got caught in the reeds or an empty boat trapped in the branches by the shore meant that for days, even weeks, it would be impossible to calm him. For years things had been quiet at the lake, even if the quiet was always only temporary, since there were plenty of opportunities to find things in the water. He had spent those years, growing old, in his boat. He went around the lake for his work, but seemed to be constantly searching in the water, along the shore, in the reeds, on the island. Everyone here thought they knew the real reason for his agitation. And yet, because of his consideration towards the children, many felt he was best left alone.

He supplied the local inns with fish and sold the rest of his catch in the town nearby. During the day he sat in his boat, and in the evenings he slipped along the shore. At night you could find him in the bars near the harbour or, again, in his boat. He was considerate and polite, but still often rowed past without saying hello, only to draw attention to himself at the next opportunity with an enthusiastic wave. This would be followed by an invitation to join him in his boat. He was so friendly that I, especially as a child, could not refuse and we took many *excursions*, as he called them. While we were together he would tell me all about his work and what he had caught that day and all that he had seen and done day in, day out, throughout the year and in all the years he had spent fishing on this lake. He talked to me, but seemed absent-minded. Then he would suddenly look at me intently and searchingly, but without ever asking about anything in particular. As we approached the island, he always grew nervous and jumpy. He broke out in a sweat, his shirt sodden, his entire body trembling, his eyes fixed on me. Only the oars kept him steady. His trembling gradually subsided and once again his expression became open, relaxed, even friendly. As if he had noticed my shock, he smiled in embarrassment and ruffled my hair. We turned and rowed back to shore, and yet, as relaxed and open as he appeared to be, he never once took his eyes off me. He seemed to be using me as a means of following his boy's trail, even finding him. I didn't want this and tried to avoid him, but couldn't. Next time he had changed and asked me about school, about my classmates and friends, their likes and dislikes. He wanted to know everything. Occasionally, he managed to convince one or the other of my friends to row out to the island with him, and he would stare at them just as intently, searching for something or maybe just remembering his son, thinking of what he might have looked like now. Whatever the reason, it was as if he had identified and understood something in each of us, so we were glad when our parents forbade us to go near him again.

He almost always had in his boat one of the children who even now and so many years later still made this area feel less safe. He taught them how to fish, something they willingly took up, and in winter he taught them to ice skate. That way he could spend time with them throughout the year. They weren't shy with him, and they trusted him. At least they appeared to. They sat in his boat with their fishing rods and let him help them up when they slipped on the ice. Yet I got the impression they tolerated rather than liked him, because more than once I saw them duck into the reeds and hide when he rowed past. He was, in any case, the inevitable witness of their secret expeditions to the island, or at the very least an accessory, since it is inconceivable that they could have slipped past him unnoticed. So they obviously agreed to sit with him in his boat every now and then to keep him from telling on them.

He would never have kept quiet about us, though. On the way out to the island we already had water in the boat, more than usual. The boat didn't belong to any of us, so no one bothered to take care of it. It had been abandoned years before, tied to a tree trunk that rose from the water. On that day the boat rode lower in the water than usual. We rowed out anyway, probably because we had the new kid with us. He had come to our school a few weeks earlier, and we took him with us to the spot where we always landed, an opening in the reeds, a clearing where we tied up. That is where I always picture him, standing there in the reeds, looking at us, wondering what we had planned for him.

All summer long they searched for the boy. They found his bicycle not far from where we had set off.

I have not set foot on the island since then, and since then the boy's father has not left the lake, and I have watched him all the years since.

We never said a word about the incident. Life went on and we still met up, but we no longer went out to the island.

I turned on the light and sat on the bed. The next morning, there were children creeping around the house. The light's on in his room, I heard one say. A moment later they were standing in the doorway and in my room, looking straight at me, bright-eyed and happy. One of them held out a box with a kitten. It had adopted them, they said. They asked for milk for the cat, and when I came back into the room, they were standing at the window. They were looking across the lake over to the island in the reeds.

Morning,
Noon and Night

The wall in front of the house had been replastered and the moss had not yet regrown to cover it like the other walls in the area. The railings were freshly painted and the hedge behind them was sparse. On top of the wall stood some candles. Streams of wax trickled down the new cement and pooled on the pavement in little puddles. Children jumped over the puddles as if they were obstacles.

Old limes and oaks lined the street. Women and children walked in their shade. Dogs roamed between the trunks followed by their owners, who stopped and waited, examining the trees' craggy bark. Then they continued on their way. Sometimes a car would brake and stop at the junction before driving on. The sound of its engine faded into the surrounding noise.

A small boy walked along the pavement holding a woman's hand. He steered his toy car along the garden wall. After a while he broke away from the woman and ran ahead, still steering his car along the wall. Whenever there was something in the car's way, he lifted it over the obstacle and set it back on the wall. Then he dragged it along the metal railings. He imitated the noise it made, humming and singing to himself, his voice rising and falling as if he were changing gears. The woman kept calling after him, but the further he went the faster he ran, until he finally rounded a corner and was gone.

An old woman had reached the junction. She stopped in front of the house and walked up and down, in a world of her own, with her arms crossed. She kept turning the corner and heading a few steps down the street. Then she stopped and stood still and turned and retraced her steps, only to return once again to the spot where she had doubled back. She straightened twigs here and there in the hedge and strayed into the garden. She was lost in thought, distracted, and whenever anyone approached her she recoiled and abruptly changed direction. Then she backed several steps away from the wall and, after a moment, stroked it with a finger.

As she did so, she began looking across the street at me. I had been watching that spot and the woman from my vantage point for a long time, and I could sense how much my presence irritated her. I didn't want to annoy her further. I crossed the street towards her, went right past her and strolled down the road.

The moss on the garden wall was dried out and yellowed and the paint was flaking off the railings. Behind it, the hedge stopped people peering into the partially overgrown garden. There were old villas, chestnut trees, beeches and willows, and sunbathing bodies on folding and reclining chairs under the trees. There were birds chirping and a smell of barbecue. Everything needs water, said a woman behind the hedge. From a verandah came the sound of a flute. One song, played over and over again, always breaking off at the same point with the same mistake repeated each time. A man's voice took up the melody and hummed and sang from that point on, correcting the mistake and falling silent. Then it all started again from the beginning.

A tram turned into the street, and a dog that had been lying before an open garden gate and barking at the passers-by sprang up and ran towards it, whimpering. There were children on the tram and a girl, who had evidently been waiting for the dog, called out a name. She beckoned him over and threw something out of the window, a soft toy. The dog raced after it and sniffed and gnawed at it. Then he took off with his trophy.

On the street, right where the soft toy had landed, skid marks ran across the tarmac. A few metres away, arrows and numbers were drawn on the road and on the pavement.

I went to him just once, and even then only because my regular GP was not available that day.

Bells from a nearby church mingled with the sound of the flute. A few gardens further on, both were drowned out by shouts from a school football pitch and the roar of the crowd when a goal was scored or missed. Flags were waved. They could just be seen over the hedge. Every now and then a ball came flying out into the road. It was quickly chased down by a child and taken back or thrown over the hedge from the pavement onto the pitch, where it was greeted with cheers.

A minor ailment had brought me to him, a scratchy throat that had bothered me for some time, nothing serious, but he took more care to examine me than any other GP I had seen.

Occasionally a child sneaked out of the play-ground into the road and climbed the garden wall. He pulled himself up on the railings and then, if he managed to reach the top of the wall, eased himself down the other side. An anxious mother always followed. She scolded the child and took him back to the park.

I stopped at the roundabout past the school and crossed to the other side to walk back from there. A removals van stood in front of a house where people were moving in and out at the same time. The van was emptied and then immediately filled again. Furniture and objects were carried out of the house and back in. A window on the top floor stood wide open. In a mirror leaning against the window, I could see the tops of the trees and the junction to which I now returned. Below the window a crow was busy picking twigs out of the gutter. Now and then it pecked at its reflection in the mirror as if trying to feed on its image, only to eventually drop every twig into the garden with a caw each time.

It's not angina, he said after probing my throat with his hands and his stethoscope. He stood up and went to a glass cabinet, unlocked it and took out a packet of pills.

Behind the fences and shrubbery, the barred ground-floor windows were half opened, their curtains swaying in the breeze. In the rooms were lamps and walls covered with books, mirrors and paintings. On the façades, sunlight and the shadows of trees. Gravel and the sound of footsteps on the gravel path approaching or moving away. There were the ferns, the bushes and the poppies. The smell of herbs and clean laundry wafted over the road on the wind.

A few streets away a roof was being stripped. A crane hovered over the rooftops, and from that direction came the sound of knocking and hammering and banging, which mingled with the yelling of the children in the park and on the football pitch. There were cars, the flute and the music from other gardens and houses. There was a whistle and a yapping dog, at which the whistle was probably directed. The school bell pealed. Screaming children answered. They poured out into the road. Some of them held hands and wandered off quickly. A girl suddenly ran out from the crowd and across the road towards me. A woman supervising the children hurried after her and grabbed her out of the road. The girl had run in front of a car. The woman now smiled apologetically at the driver who returned the smile before setting off again. The woman held the girl with both hands, shook her, hugged her, ruffled her hair and led her back to the others, who had missed the drama.

I approached the junction again and noticed that the old woman I had avoided earlier was still walking up and down in front of the house. A nun was watching her from the convent across the road. The nun had also been keeping an eye on me for some time. She now closed the window, and soon after she joined me on the pavement. I was in no mood to talk, and so I turned away. She crossed the road and went over to the woman.

People have been coming here for weeks, she said, nodding at the recently repaired wall.

The woman seemed not to want to hear anything. She lowered her head reluctantly, turned and walked away in the opposite direction. Her arms were tightly crossed, and she walked more quickly than before. The nun stared after her and then finally gave up. She returned to the convent, but not without checking once more whether I wanted to talk with her.

I went over to the junction. I waited there for a while in case the old woman returned, but she didn't.

Marks for laying cable glowed on the tarmac and only now did I notice the small tree on the corner. Tied to a stake, it grew crookedly out of a low hedge.

There were the new wall, the railings, the hedge, and behind them the gravel path leading to the house and to a flight of steps. At the top of the steps a stone lion guarded the front door.

They say his mother was in the car with him and his wife. I thought of that now, and of the three crosses he had drawn for me on the packet of pills for *morning*, *noon* and *night*.

You Don't Know Them,
They're Strangers

On his front door, he read the name they had called him all evening. He entered the flat and it seemed familiar, but also strange, as if something had changed during the time he had spent with his neighbours. Some things were missing and some things hadn't been there before. He couldn't say what belonged to him and what didn't, nor did he have the slightest idea how he could possibly work that out. The more he looked around the room, the less he could tell.

He stepped outside the front door again and again, but the name on it remained the same.

He rang the neighbours' doorbell and woke them up with the excuse that he had forgotten something. What he had left behind could not be found, but they did find the pictures they had spoken about earlier. The ones they had wanted to show him. He looked through them now. They were old photographs, and the year printed on the back showed they had been taken at a time when he could not have known his two neighbours.

And yet, one of the faces in the pictures exactly matched the face staring back at him from the mirror.

He gave up and lay down on the bed. A phone call interrupted his thoughts. A stranger who claimed to be his friend absolutely had to see him that night. That very moment, in fact.

When he walked into the bar, he had no idea whom he was supposed to meet. Nor did he know how he was meant to recognize this so-called friend. Yet the friend was there, waiting, and beckoned him over to his table.

From the first sentence, it was clear that this man also took him for the person his neighbours believed him to be. After a while the stranger was as familiar to him as if they had been childhood friends. This friend even knew his past though they hadn't spoken about it.

Back at his flat, the earlier disarray had now become a familiar order. Everything was in its place, at least so it seemed. He got his bearings and closed his eyes, confident that when he reopened them, everything would be as it should.

The next morning, he set off for the office in an area he had never been in before. Or maybe he had, it was hard to tell. He entered the office, greeted his colleagues and was greeted in return. He sat at a desk he sensed was *his* desk, but he was far from certain. He asked questions and was asked questions and gave answers. He made some calls, drafted letters and signed documents as if he had never done anything else.

Hours later his neighbour greeted him as if for the first time and said that she and her husband were looking forward to getting to know him and to becoming good neighbours.

The name on his door was not the same one he had signed on letters in the office. He went into the flat. What he discovered was new, different from what he remembered had been there that morning. Once again he looked through the wardrobes and cupboards for documents and compared his face to the picture on the identity card, which looked exactly like him.

The doorbell rang and a woman was standing in the room. She had come to pick him up. She knew that otherwise he would have kept her waiting again or not shown up at all. She had been trying to reach him all day. They needed to talk, now. He didn't know the woman, but they talked things out. Just when he thought she had calmed down and they were back on track, she announced that it was all over. He agreed and so they split up. He took her home and returned to his flat.

This happened often now. The names on his door kept changing. Each morning he left his flat and was recognized, even if not as the person he thought he was at the time. People knew who he was meant to be, or at least seemed to know. He was whoever they wanted to see in him. Without any effort or subterfuge, and no matter how he behaved, he always seemed to meet their expectations.

For a while he responded to people only hesitantly, since they always had the better of him, but he soon overcame what seemed like memory lapses or absent-mindedness. With each encounter he found it easier to adapt to every new situation. People took him to be the one they perceived, and he became the one they expected him to be. Without disguising himself, he went around disguised, if not from others then simply from himself.

Through all the changes, his flat remained the same. At least the address stayed the same. His neighbours stayed the same, all the other people seemed to stay the same. Only *his* life seemed to redefine itself each day.

More and more often, he enjoyed ringing the doorbell at a strange address to see who he would be at that moment for that particular stranger. It could go well or badly because there was no way of knowing if the door would be opened in a friendly way or slammed shut in his face. He didn't know if he would be greeted as an acquaintance, as an unwelcome stranger or as an enemy whose presence would be considered rude or even offensive.

When he awoke at night or in the morning and couldn't tell whether or not the flat had changed yet, he would look in his address book for the name of someone with whom he had made plans the night before, and sometimes that person would have no idea what he was talking about.

Once, in a sort of relapse, he was taken for the person he might have been before this all started. At least that was his impression, and he was surprised by the warmth with which people greeted him. They thought he had returned after a long absence. Still, when he went back to his flat immediately after that experience, hoping to find it restored to the way it had been, he stood there, feeling indifferent. The flat belonged to him, but at the same time it didn't, and everything continued on its new course.

It usually occurred at night, while he was asleep. At least it did for a long time, but then it began to happen more often during the day. And when he returned to his flat in the evening or even earlier, it was impossible to predict whether he would re-enter the flat as the salesman who had left it that morning or as the estate agent in whose guise he had just sold a piece of property, or even as the GP who had just chatted up a woman.

A shard of memory remained each time, at least for a while, or perhaps just a sense of previous possibilities and limitations. He was at the mercy of his strengths and weaknesses because it always took him a while to recognize them as his own. They became more and more difficult to cope with. He worried that he would lose perspective and no longer be aware of what was happening to him. But he didn't need to worry, at least not on account of others, because *they* knew whom they were dealing with. Or maybe they didn't. In any case, he eventually took things as they came and no longer saw his condition as a disadvantage. He began to enjoy going out and, by meeting others, meeting in himself someone he didn't know.

Ever more frequently, from one moment to the next, constantly, continuously, seamlessly, no matter where he was or where he tried to hide, he was discovered, recognized and confronted, and things took their course. On one and the same day he married and stood, an old man, at his wife's grave, only to find himself the next moment in a divorce court believing he had got off lightly. Hours later he found himself unable to cope with the loss. He became a happy father and could not bear the thought of having children. He was a student attending the school in which he taught. He performed surgery and woke from anaesthesia. He raised bees, fell in love, mourned, was afraid and frightened others, and was happy. He was finally alone and intolerably lonely. He couldn't decide which car he wanted to buy. Then he pawned his television and wore his last frayed shirt. And so on, constantly, continuously, without interruption. It exhausted him, wore him out. He tried to cope by staying in his flat. But he went out because he had to conform to the needs, desires and aspirations of the person whose life he was living at that moment. He withdrew more frequently now, every day, every night, into his flat, his bed, burrowing himself in there and refusing to get up or to do anything other than sleep, regardless of whose dreams he would have to dream. He did not want to wake up. But he did wake up and get up, which he in fact wanted to do since there were things he had planned, even though they were thwarted by the very first encounter of the day.

By now, he also felt at home at other addresses, and what at first had seemed to happen by chance was now routine.

He entered a building to visit someone, but was stopped by a man who took him for a neighbour and held the lift for him. He got out one floor above the man and went to the flat where someone was meant to be waiting for him, but no one was home. He put the key in the lock, the door opened, and he realized that this flat, too, belonged to him.

After glancing around, he left the building and went along the streets, peering into windows. When he saw windows that were dark, he went into the building and hid in the flat for a while, which then became his flat.

He didn't return to his own flat for a long time after that night. He moved to new areas, towns and cities, and his key fitted the lock of any door he wished to open. Yet he wanted to return to the place where it all began, to be closer to his own history. At least that is what he thought, regardless of whose flat it might have been or whose life he had lived at the time, or was living now.

Out 2012

Peirene

Contemporary European Literature. Thought provoking, well designed, short.

"Two-hour books to be devoured in a single sitting: literary cinema for those fatigued by film." TLS

Online Bookshop
Literary Salons
Reading Guides
Meike's Blog: The Pain and Passion of a Small Publisher

www.peirenepress.com

Follow us on twitter and Facebook @PeirenePress
Peirene Press is building a community of passionate readers.
We love to hear your comments and ideas.
Please e-mail the publisher at: meike.ziervogel@peirenepress.com